Jakers!™

Piggley and the Magic Doll

adapted by Laura Driscoll
images by Entara Ltd.

SIMON SPOTLIGHT
New York   London   Toronto   Sydney

Hello, there. I'm Grandpa Piggley. Gather round and I'll tell you a story about when I was growing up down on Raloo Farm. *Jakers!* What fun we used to have . . .

Based on the TV series *Jakers! The Adventures of Piggley Winks* created by Entara Ltd.

SIMON SPOTLIGHT
An imprint of Simon & Schuster Children's Publishing Division
1230 Avenue of the Americas, New York, New York 10020
SIMON SPOTLIGHT and colophon are registered trademarks of Simon & Schuster, Inc.
Manufactured in the United States of America
2 4 6 8 10 9 7 5 3
ISBN-13: 978-0-689-87611-0
ISBN-10: 0-689-87611-4

One sunny day on Raloo Farm, Piggley and his friends Ferny and Dannan were having a contest to see whose top would spin longer: Piggley's Tip Topper or Ferny's Red Tornado.

Even Piggley's little sister, Molly, and her pet fawn, Sweets, were eager to see who would win.

They were all so distracted that they didn't notice a truck driving by the farm just then. The truck hit a bump in the road. *BUMP!*
Something sprang out of the back of the truck. It bounced off Piggley's head and landed in Molly's hands.

"It's a doll!" Molly exclaimed. "A leprechaun doll!" She hugged it tightly. "And it came to *me*!" Molly decided to name it Babby, and ran off to play with the doll.

But Piggley, Ferny, and Dannan thought it was very strange—had a doll really just fallen out of the sky?

"Maybe it isn't a doll. Maybe it's a real leprechaun!" Piggley suggested.
"Or maybe it is a real leprechaun just *pretending* to be a doll."
  "What?" Dannan exclaimed in shock. "And why would he be doing that?"

"Because he doesn't want us to see where he's hidden his pot of gold!" Piggley replied.

Ferny gasped. "Janey Mack!" he cried. "Do you really think so, Piggley?"

Piggley wasn't sure, but he wanted to find out!

Piggley couldn't wait to find out more about the leprechaun. So at bedtime that night Piggley borrowed his mother's book on leprechauns, and began to read.

"Leprechauns are excellent shoemakers," Piggley read. "But they only make one shoe—never a pair. Hmm . . . ," Piggley kept reading. "When he's finished making shoes, the leprechaun always makes a delicious feast."

Piggley read and read. Soon his head was spinning with leprechaun lore. He needed a drink of milk to help him get to sleep. So he headed into the kitchen with a flashlight in his hand.

But suddenly, Piggley forgot all about the milk.

There before him was a shiny, very new-looking boot—*one* boot.

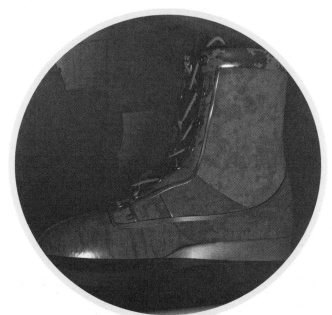

And the kitchen table was covered with freshly baked pies! "The book said a leprechaun makes a feast when he's finished making shoes!" Piggley said with a gasp.

He was convinced: Molly's doll was a leprechaun for sure!

The next morning Piggley was determined to find out where that leprechaun was hiding his gold. Piggley, Ferny, and Dannan watched as Molly put her doll down for a nap. Suddenly a gust of wind blew the doll's blanket away. Molly chased after it.

"She's gone, Piggley!" whispered Ferny. "Now you can get the doll!"

Hanging from a tree branch over the doll's buggy, Piggley stretched and grasped the doll between his feet—just as a flock of sheep passed by.

"Whooooooaaaa!" Piggley exclaimed as he lost his grip and got carried away on the backs of the sheep.

The doll went flying—and landed, safe and sound, back in the buggy.

Piggley decided the only way to get the doll was to make a deal with Molly. She could play with his favorite spinning top, Tip Topper, if he could play with her doll.

"Okay," Molly said as she ran off happily with Piggley's top.

At last Piggley had captured the leprechaun!

"Okay, leprechaun," said Piggley. "Where's your pot of gold?"

The leprechaun did not answer, so Ferny asked. "Please tell us," he begged. But nothing they said could get the leprechaun to talk.

"Well, if you ask me," said Dannan, "he's not even a real leprechaun." Piggley hated to admit it, but he thought Dannan might be right. "Maybe he is just a doll," Piggley said with a sigh.

CLINK! Suddenly a coin fell from the doll's pocket onto the floor.

"Jakers!" Piggley exclaimed. He had read about this in the book. "Every leprechaun carries a piece of gold in his pocket, but if someone else sees it, it changes into a regular coin!"

Piggley, Dannan, and Ferny stared at the doll. "So you *are* a real leprechaun!" said Ferny.

"A real leprechaun?" Molly asked when Piggley shared their discovery.
"That's right," said Piggley. "But he won't tell us where his pot of gold is buried."

"Babby is too little to talk yet," Molly said. "But maybe one of his friends can tell you!"

Piggley, Ferny, and Dannan looked at one another, confused. "Friends?" asked Ferny.

"Come on, follow me," said Molly.

Molly took them to the window of the store in town.

"I've never seen so many leprechauns in my life!" said Ferny.

Dannan sighed. "They're not leprechauns, Ferny," she said. "They're dolls—just like Molly's doll!"

Piggley was not so sure. "But he can't be a doll," he said. "What about the pies . . . and the one shiny shoe? What about the gold coin in his pocket?"

"I put that coin in Babby's pocket today," Molly said. "Dad gave it to me for helping him take Mammie's pies to the market."

Piggley looked shocked. "*Mammie* baked those pies?"

"Uh-huh," said Molly. "And Dad had to get some boot polish because he had enough for only one boot."

Ferny and Dannan began to giggle.

Piggley felt a little bit embarrassed. The doll *was* just a doll. Piggley realized that he had made up his mind about something too quickly, without making sure he had all the facts.

He promised himself never to do that again.

Then, his lesson learned, Piggley joined his friends in having a good, long laugh.